Half a World Away

"Coo-ee, Lou-ee."

Library of Congress Cataloging-in-Publication Data • Gleeson, Libby. • [Amy and Louis] • Half a world away / by Libby Gleeson ; illustrated by Freya Blackwood. • 1st American ed. • p. cm. • Previously published under title: Amy and Louis. • Summary: When Louie's best friend Amy moves to the other side of the world, Louie must find a way to reconnect with her. • ISBN-13: 978-0-439-88977-3 / ISBN-10: 0-439-88977-4 • [1. Best friends–Fiction. 2. Friendship–Fiction. 3. Moving, Household–Fiction.] I. Blackwood, Freya, ill. II. Title. • PZ7.G48148Hal 2007 • [E]–dc22 • 2006007712 • 10 9 8 7 6 5 4 3 2 1   07 08 09 10 11 • Printed in Malaysia 46 • First American edition, March 2007

Half a World Away

By LIBBY GLEESON

Illustrated by FREYA BLACKWOOD

Arthur A. Levine Books 🏮 An Imprint of Scholastic Inc.

Amy and Louie built towers as high as the sky.
They dug holes deep enough to bury bears,
and they saw magical creatures in clouds.

When Amy was in the sandbox
and Louie was on the swing,
she called to him across the yard
with the special word her mother taught her.

"Coo-ee, Lou-ee!"

Louie always came to play.

When Louie was in the dressing-up corner
and Amy was with the play dough,
he called to her across the room
with the same special word.

"Coo-ee, Am-ee!"

Amy always came to play.

And when they were at home, they called
to each other across the fence. "Coo-ee, Lou-ee."

"Coo-ee, Am-ee." One of them would soon come climbing through the gap with secrets to share.

But one day Amy and her family moved
a long, long way away . . .

. . . to the other side of the world.

Louie stopped building towers,
digging holes, and staring at clouds.
He no longer called to anyone
across the yard, the room, or the fence.

He thought about Amy every day and every night.

In the place where Amy was,
there was nowhere to dig holes or build towers,
and the clouds held only raindrops.

She thought about Louie every night and every day.

"If I call Amy really loudly,
she'll hear me, won't she?"
Louie asked his mom.

His mom shook her head. "Amy is too far away," she said.
"When you are awake in the day, she is asleep at night."

"If I call Amy really, really
loudly, she'll hear me,
won't she?" he asked his dad.

His dad shook his head. "Amy is half the world away," he said.
"When she is awake in the day, you are asleep at night."

"If I call Amy with the loudest
call anyone could ever, ever do,
she'll hear me, won't she?"
he asked his grandma.

"Maybe," his grandma said.
"You can only try."

So Louie spread his arms as wide as he could
and threw back his head.

His cry rang out across the yard,
across the street,
and past the edge of the town.

Louie fell back and stared up at the sky
where clouds were making strange seahorses
and wild, wild dragons.

Across the ocean,
in a city where tall buildings
stretched to the sky,
Amy woke and came sleepily
to breakfast.

"I had a lovely dream," she said.
"I dreamt about Louie
and he called me."

Half a world away,
Louie slept,
smiling in his dream.